Invasion
of the
Bunny-Wunnies

by Steven Butler
Illustrated by Bill Ledger

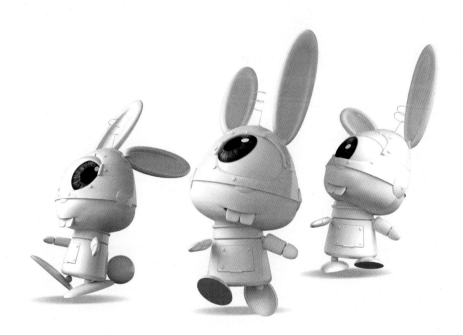

Houghton Mifflin Harcourt.

In this story ...

Ann

(Boost)

Ann is super strong. She has the power to lift boulders.

Ben
(Sprint)

Evan
(Flex)

Miss Linen
(teacher)

Miss Baker
(lunch helper)

Ann marched into Hero Academy feeling very happy with herself.

Ben and Evan were watching television.

"I did it!" Ann said. "I rescued Lexis City!"

"What was your mission?" asked Ben.

"To defeat a giant squid," Ann replied. "I threw it back into the sea."

"Good work," said Evan, "but I think you should fix your cape."

Ann looked down. There was a tear in her cape.

Ann groaned. "I don't like sewing," she said. "I always break the needle or snap the thread." "You just need to practice," Ben replied. Ann sighed. "I know, but I'd rather go on another mission."

Just then, they heard a strange noise in the corridor.
HOP, BOING, HOP, BOING.
They all peeked out ... and gasped.

The hallway was full of bunnies.
"How did Ray Ranter's bunny-wunnies get in?"
Ann asked.
"I haven't got a clue," Ben replied.

Bunny-Wunnies

Bunny-wunnies are robotic rabbits. They were invented by Ray Ranter to help him with his dastardly plans. Ray Ranter is an enemy of Hero Academy.

Ray Ranter

NUMBER 1 MOST WANTED VILLAIN

paws that can turn into saws, umbrellas, and other attachments

front pouch

Miss Baker came running out of the kitchen carrying a cookbook. "It's a nightmare!" she cried. "The bunny-wunnies want to steal the instructions for my power pancakes."

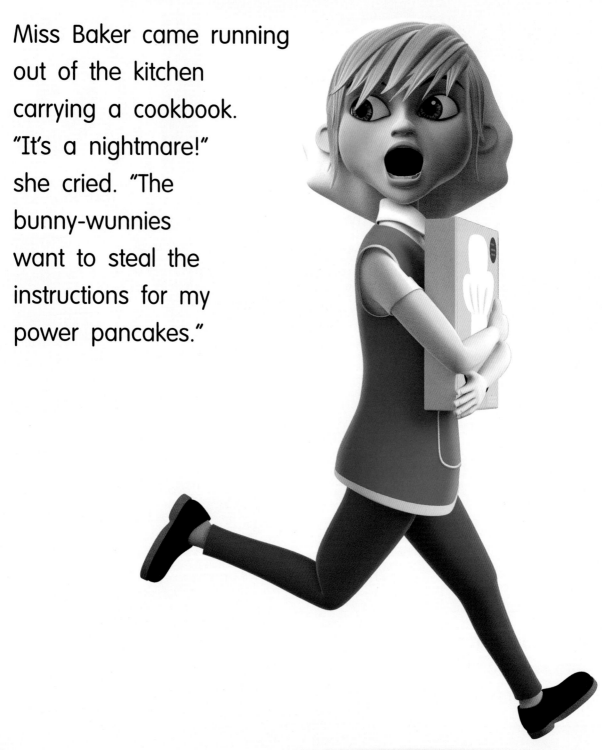

The bunnies saw the cookbook and started to chase Miss Baker. She screamed and ran off.

"We have to stop them," said Ben. "Let's round those bunnies up!"

"I'll help you," said Ann, grabbing a bunny-wunny. "Me too," said Evan. He stretched his arms out. Ben ran round in circles and chased the bunny-wunnies into Evan's arms.

The bunnies pushed against Evan's arms.
"I can't hold them forever!" he said. "We need
a super-strong net."

Ann knew just what to do! She raced to the gym and grabbed some rope.

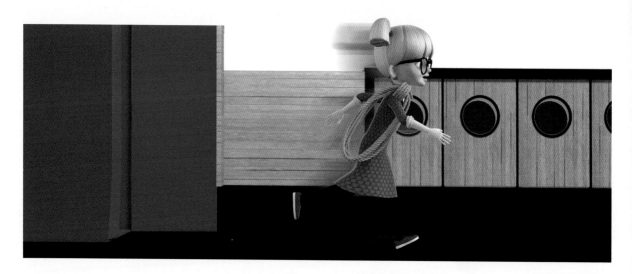

Then she picked up a metal chair and broke off one of its legs.

Ann bent the chair leg into a needle shape.
Then she stitched the rope into a super-strong net.

Ann ran back down the hall.

Evan was still trying to hold on to all the bunny-wunnie

"Hurry!" he yelled.

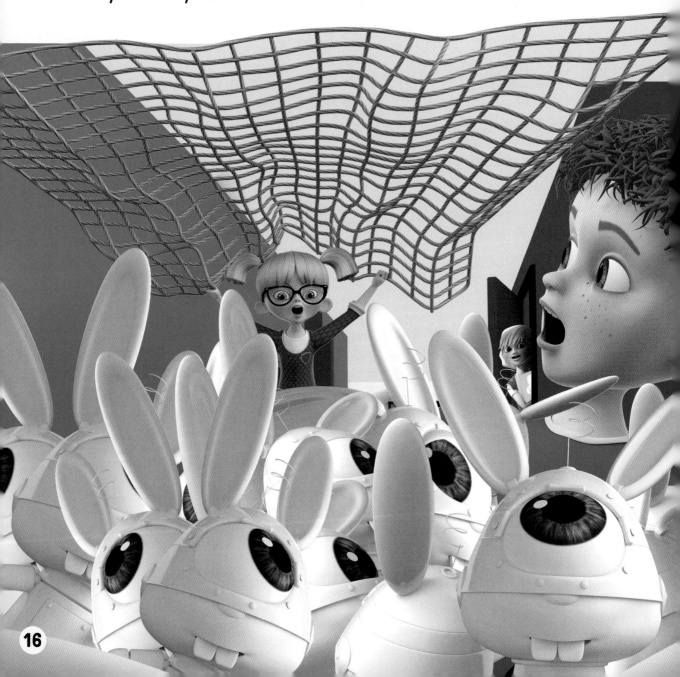

Ann threw the net over the bunny-wunnies.
Then she slung it over her shoulder.
"Naughty bunnies!" she said.

"Let's put the bunny-wunnies outside," Miss Baker replied.

They took the net of bunny-wunnies out to the school field.

"How are we going to get rid of them?" asked Ann.
Suddenly, they heard a helicopter.
"It's Ray Ranter!" yelled Ben.

A huge grabber dropped down from the helicopter and snatched up the net. Then the helicopter headed off in the direction of Ranter Tower.

Ann let out a sigh of relief. "That's the last we'll see of those annoying bunny-wunnies … for now," she said.

"That was a great net, Ann," Ben said, as they watched the helicopter disappear. "Nice stitching." Ann smiled. "That reminds me … there's something else I need to stitch!"

Later …

Ann was in the classroom. She had just finished
stitching up the tear in her cape.

"Good work, Ann!" said Miss Linen. "Your stitching is
much better."

"I've had some practice!" replied Ann, with a grin.

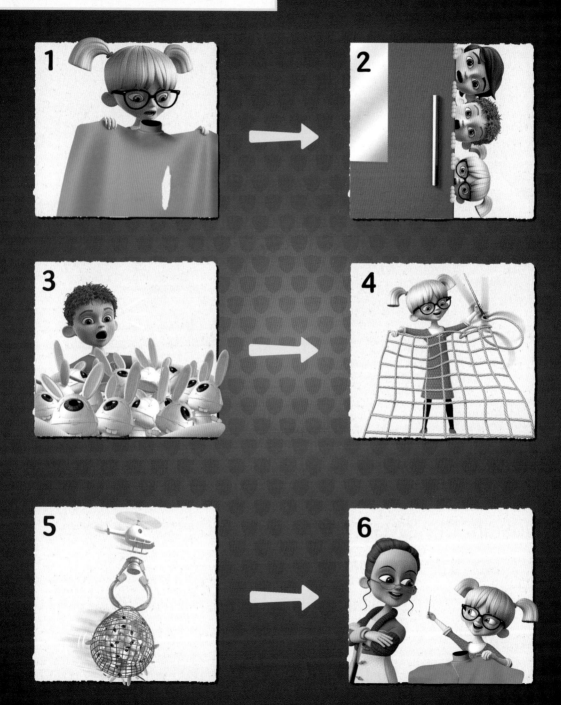